MW00915930

For Father Christmas and his helpers

First published in Great Britain in 1996 by Sapling,
an imprint of Boxtree Limited, 25 Eccleston Place,
London SW1W 9NF.

10 9 8 7 6 5 4 3

ISBN: 0 7522 2285 6

Originated by Loudwater
Printed and bound in Italy by L.E.G.O.

A CIP catalogue entry is available from any British Library.

Watch out for Father Christmas!

by

Kate Veale

sapling

It was the day before Christmas Eve. The light was fading and lamps were being switched on all over the town, shining out across the snow. If you looked closely through the winter night you could see, behind frosty breaths, Oliver Otter and his three friends, Will Squirrel, Digsby the Mole and Drew the Shrew. They were on their way to listen to carols around the big Christmas tree in the town square.

As they listened, Drew looked up through the lighted branches to the top of the buildings edging the square. One of these had a stone statue of a kneeling deer on its gable. The stone deer flicked a flake of snow from its ear.

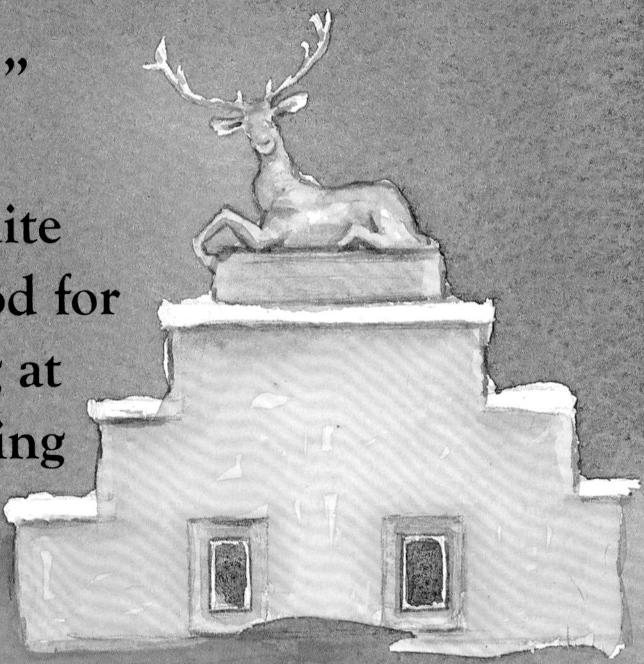

"That deer moved!" exclaimed Drew.

The others, not quite believing him, stood for a long time staring at the deer, but nothing happened. They gave up and set off for home.

"I'm sure I saw the deer move," said Drew as they walked back through the snow.

When the four friends were out of sight, the deer stretched up on its hind legs, then onto its forelegs, and lightly stepped down the gable and across the rooftops: it had work to do.

Christmas lights were on and the shop windows were bright. Well wrapped up against the cold, people stood choosing presents or hurried along laughing on their way to warm homes. No one noticed a quick shadow high above them softly moving across the rooftops against the night sky.

The four friends reached Oliver Otter's home and, after stamping the snow from their boots, went inside. They made hot drinks and sat around the log fire toasting their faces and hands in the warmth. Drew sat on the fender staring into the fire and watching the flames crackling and flickering up the chimney. He was thinking about the deer. "I'm going back again!" he announced, suddenly. "Are you coming?"

EXTRA
STRONG
POPCORN

Wearing extra jumpers, vests, two hats, ski socks and woolly boots, Oliver, Will and Digsby followed Drew through the snow back to the town square. The gable was empty.
"It's gone!" Drew squeaked, excitedly.
"Come on," said Will, "up the drainpipe to the roof."
Will bounded up carrying his inflatable ball and rope invention so that the others could be pulled up behind him. Digsby decided to climb up inside the pipe as he didn't like heights, but he could tunnel along anything. They clambered onto the gable.

"Follow the deer tracks in the snow," said Drew. So they set off, up and down the snowy rooftops. At last, climbing to a ridge and peering around a chimney, they saw it. The deer was standing on a window ledge gently tapping the glass with his antlers.
As they watched, a child opened the window and sleepily pushed what looked like a scrap of paper into a drawstring bag the deer had around his neck. After stroking the deer's muzzle and hugging him goodbye, the child shut the window.
With one magnificent leap the deer landed lightly on the next window ledge and the whole process was repeated.
"I told you it moved," whispered Drew to himself, his eyes wide in amazement.

They shrank back into the shadows of the chimney as the deer passed by, a flash of movement blocking out the snow and then it was gone. A piece of paper fluttered to the ground.

"What does it say?" asked the others as Drew picked it up.

"Oh no!" said Oliver reading the note. "It's a present list from two children for Father Christmas, and the deer has dropped it. They won't get their presents now!"

"Yes they will," said Drew. "I've got a plan." He put the list in his pocket and they clambered back across the rooftops towards home.

The next day was Christmas Eve. As the clock struck eleven, the four friends hurried from the house towards the square. They arrived breathless and looked up to the rooftop once more. The deer was still there!

"We're not too late!" cried Digsby, and they climbed up to the gable, approaching the deer slowly. Drew stroked the stone muzzle and they climbed carefully onto the deer's back. The deer didn't move.

"Do you really think this is one of Father Christmas's reindeer?" asked Digsby after they had been sitting there for a while. No one answered. But there were four very cold bottoms sitting on the stone deer as the clock struck half past midnight.

"Father Christmas is not going to come after all," said Digsby, sadly.

Suddenly they could hear the distant jingling of bells and the deer moved beneath them. At first they couldn't tell where the noise was coming from, then an enormous sleigh and Father Christmas appeared on the roof next to them. All the reindeer were stamping hooves, and blowing billows of frosty breath into the air.

"Hello!" said Father Christmas thrusting his whiskery face towards them. "What have we here?"

"We've come to help!" whispered Drew.

“Good,” exclaimed Father Christmas moving his face away as he quickly harnessed up the deer to the other reindeer. “I can always do with some help on my busiest night.” He jumped back onto his sleigh and they were off into the dark, bells jangling at every step. “Faster deers! Faster!” shouted Father Christmas cheerily, and to the four friends he said, “we will go around the world tonight. This is the night that time stands still!”

And it did, whilst they delivered presents to every child who had made a list. They even completed the job more quickly than usual because Drew wasn’t as fat as Father Christmas and didn’t have to squeeze himself down the chimneys.

At last they had finished! Then Drew pulled out the present list, which he had almost forgotten in his excitement, and read ...
"One magnum red Ferrari and one perfect prince in a castle."
"Impossible! Isn't there something a bit smaller?"

"What!!" exclaimed Father Christmas. "I think we'd better just give them a medium sized magic box, and then they can have whatever fits into that!" he laughed.
Drew delivered the presents, leaving them at the foot of the children's beds.

sorry ~ no
Ponies
F.C. x

As daylight approached, Father Christmas's job was completed for another year and the four friends waved from the door step.
"Goodbye Father Christmas, goodbye deer, see you next year," they called out as the sleigh disappeared into the morning sky.
All four fell straight to sleep, and when they awoke it was Christmas Day!
"Do you think it was just a dream?"
asked Oliver looking out of the window. But he could see deer tracks quite clearly in the snow leading across the rooftops ...

... So whenever you see a stone deer in a town nearby, and you think it moves, you might just be right, especially on those nights before Christmas.

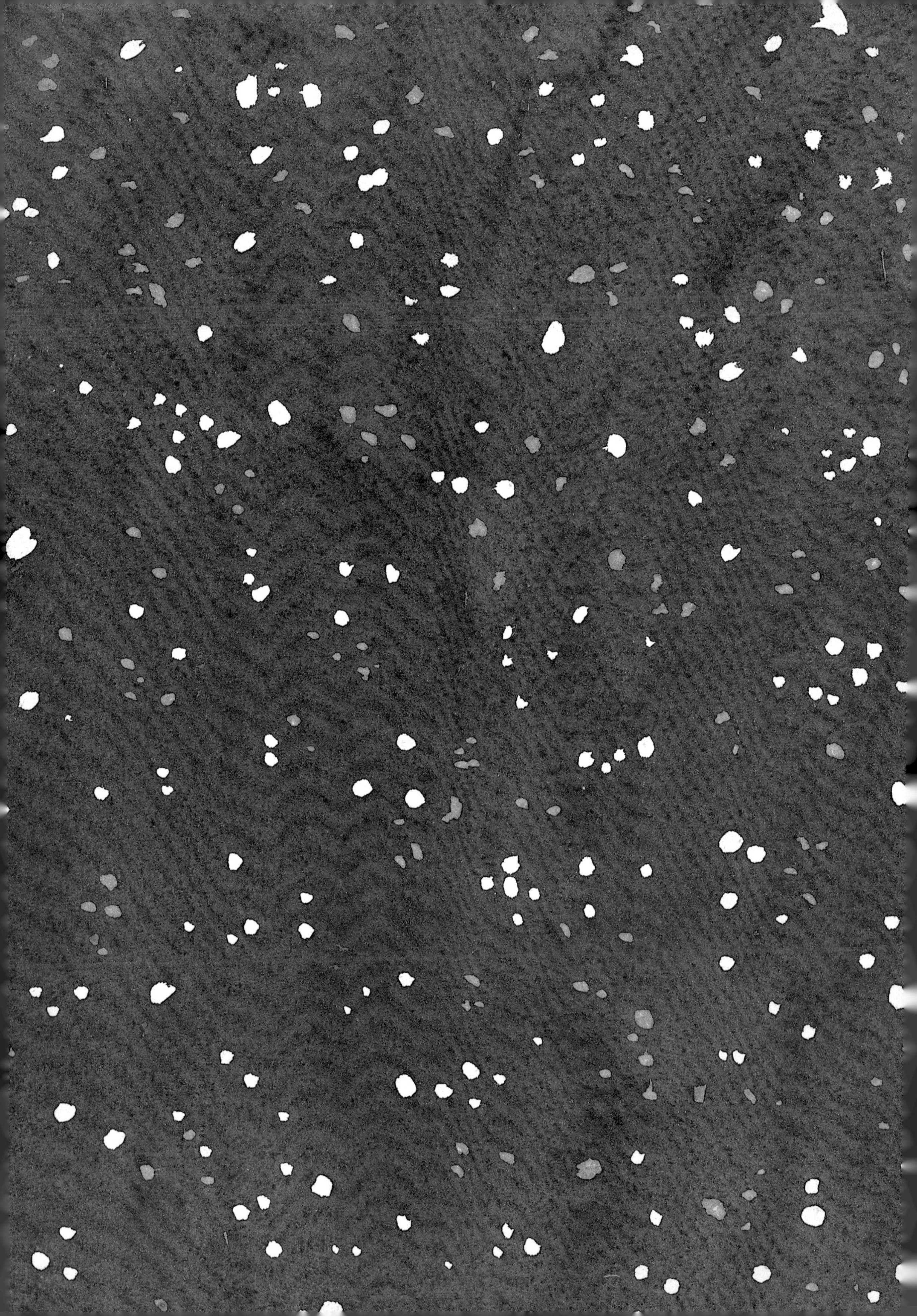